Table of Contents

MW00444967

Preface and Introduction

Preface. Volunteers and bivocationals represent the largest segment of music leadership in most churches today. Some of these volunteer and bivocational leaders have had some formal training in church music leadership skills; however, the vast majority have had little or no training in either basic music or basic ministry skills.

For this reason, many churches have not experienced any change in years in their type of music or style of worship. Many sing from a narrow repertoire of hymnic literature passed from generation to generation. While this transfer of local church music heritage is laudable, the failure of churches to incorporate music which interests and appeals to more contemporary generations has alienated many would-be congregant singers. The music used in many of today's churches has lost its ability to hold the interest of those for whom its message is intended.

Or has it? Is the music at fault, or could the primary culprit be a lack of understanding about how to best use hymns and choruses (both old and new) in worship? Perhaps the problem lies more in the method of presentation and use in worship than in the choice of music.

A better understanding of the hymnal and its contents will help music leaders to increase their knowledge and skill in using the hymnal. To that end this book is offered.

Introduction. It has been said that "variety's the very spice of life."[1] While most of us take comfort in a certain amount of stability and predictability, variety adds interest and vitality to an otherwise mundane existence. Think for a moment about how variety affects the various parts of your life. What would it be like to eat only one food, listen to one type of music, have only one choice of car to drive, or one style of house in which to live? Suppose there were no choices in the kind of work you could do, the places you could go on vacation, or the kind of books you could read. What would it be like if we couldn't choose our own doctor, or if all churches were alike, with only one style of worship? Life and all its experiences would be dull indeed.

There is another saying that "familiarity breeds contempt."[2] Without a certain amount of variety in what we do or experience, even things we enjoy doing become less enjoyable. This is true in every area of life, including our worship experiences. If worship is a repetitive act of sameness (absolute predictability), then the risk exists of our senses becoming dulled, thus altering our response to the stimuli of an encounter with God through the worship experience.

In many churches the method and manner of "doing the music" has remained constant for years. The same few hymns have been sung and accompanied in pretty much the same way since they were first introduced. That's what this book is all about: creating variety in congregational singing.

Because the hymnal is the basic music resource in thousands of churches, it stands to reason that hymn singing should be as varied and interesting as possible. Worship should provide experiences in which every person has an opportunity to respond to the message of the gospel through various avenues, including the stimulus and message of hymns, choruses, gospel songs, and other worship music.

Since congregational singing provides the greatest opportunity for involving every person present, the music selected should be presented in as interesting and varied a way as possible. Individual tastes in music vary widely. These preferences are brought into the worship experience every week. Variety in worship music can provide some of the best opportunities for reaching and involving those complacent, or uninvolved, singers in your congregation.

The hymnal contains much more than the hymns you sing each week. Being awareness of, and understanding how to use, the worship aids and indices iin your hymnal will help you discover the full potential of the hymnal. This book will also help you explore new ways of singing the hymns you sing throughout the year.

The Baptist Hymnal, 1991, (or *The Christian Praise Hymnal*) are the hymnals used in this study. If your church does not use either of these, you may want to purchase one for reference as you study this book. Both are available from Baptist Book Stores and Lifeway Christian Stores, or by calling 1-800-458-2772. If you do not wish to use these hymnals, the hymn numbers can be adapted to the numbers in the hymnal with which you are most familiar.

Refer to this book as you plan worship experiences through music for your congregation. Use the ideas presented throughout the book, along with your own creativity, to develop exciting and meaningful congregational music experiences. The better you understand each new technique before using it in worship, the more confidence you will have in leading it.

---

[1]William Cowper, *The Task.*
[2]Aesop, *The Fox and the Lion.*

Permission is granted to copy the plan sheets included in this book for your own use in developing worship services, hymn medleys, and hymn treatments.

THE
VOLUNTEER/BIVOCATIONAL
MUSIC LEADER

A GUIDE TO USING THE HYMNAL CREATIVELY

DANNY R. JONES

CONVENTION PRESS
NASHVILLE, TENNESSEE

© Copyright 1995 • Convention Press
Reprinted 1996
All Rights Reserved

5120-15

This book is the text for course 10089 in the subject area
Church Music of the Church Study Course

ISBN 0-8054-9631-9
Dewey Decimal Classification Number: 782.27
Subject Headings: Hymns—Study and Teaching

Printed in the United States of America

Church Leadership Services Division
The Sunday School Board of the Southern Baptist Convention
127 Ninth Avenue, North
Nashville, Tennessee 37234

PRODUCTION STAFF

Connie Powell and Deborah Hickerson, *textual editing*
Crystal Waters Mangrum, *music editor*
Tom Seale, *graphic designer*
M. Lester McCullough, *manager*
Mark Blankenship, *director*
MUSIC DEPARTMENT OF THE CHURCH LEADERSHIP SERVICES DIVISION

Acknowledgements

Although this book has my name on it, it is by no means the exclusive work or idea of one person. Through the years, many different persons have contributed directly or indirectly to my own knowledge and skill in the ministry of church music—teachers, poets, music leaders from churches of all sizes, accompanists, pastors, and others. The combined years of experience and knowledge of these friends in the ministry has contributed immeasurably to my understanding of the music ministry. To begin to list each person would take several pages. But to each who encouraged such a book, and to all who indirectly helped to fill the pages, goes my deep personal appreciation. Finally, I want to express a special debt of gratitude to my family—Bettye, Jeremy, and Jonathan—which constantly and freely gives its love and encouragement in these endeavors. To them goes my deepest, and continuing, love and appreciation.

Suggestions for Worship Planning

Of all the activities offered in a church, none is more important than worship. Yet, worship planning often receives the least amount of time or attention from music leaders. Whether or not your church has a choir, the worship services you plan or help to plan can enhance the total ministry of the church. Here are some suggestions for your consideration as you plan for worship.

Be Creative

Does the repetitious nature of the order of worship, or the feeling of "sameness" sometimes distract you from worshiping? If it does, imagine what it may do for the members of your congregation. Be creative in your approach to worship planning. In how many ways can a hymn be used in a service? Must the call to worship always be sung? Must the piano and organ always accompany each stanza? Take a musical survey of the congregation to discover what God has placed in your church. Become aware of the musical resources of your community as well. Several of these resources (band, orchestra, community choral groups, as well as other musicians and groups) may be available to your church if asked. Think creatively!

Be Flexible

Even when you have planned an order of worship, there may be times when your congregation needs something different. Be sensitive to the needs of your church or to a change in the sermon topic. As changes are made prior to or during a service, develop a plan for communicating these changes to your accompanists. The better you are able to anticipate changes, the easier it will be to make modifications to an existing plan. Some music leaders make it a practice to have a Plan B ready just in case what was originally planned cannot be done. A good example of this is when what the choir rehearsed earlier in the week cannot be done on Sunday because of fewer singers.

Be Functional

Do you know why you do each thing in your worship service? Do the members of your congregation know? Each part of the order of service should serve some specific purpose. If you are uncertain about why you do certain things, your church members, and certainly most guests, may be even more uncertain. Gain an understanding of the various parts of the worship service by discussing the entire service with your pastor and other worship leaders. It's very likely that several items listed in your order of worship are not worship-related at all. These may include announcements and greeting of guests, or other activities. Consider whether these enhance your worship time or detract from the real purpose of the worship experience. Could some of these activities be done prior to or following the worship service itself? These questions should be discussed by all worship leaders and/or the worship committee (if your church has one).

Be Urgent

Nothing is more important than the worship of God. Helping your people worship is your most important task. In your role as the music leader in your church, allow for periods of quality, uninterrupted time each week to plan adequately for worship services. Break out of the Wednesday/Sunday/Sunday/Wednesday time trap of planning your services. (See Long-Range below.)

Be Long-range

If you are currently planning your worship services one week at a time, consider moving to a monthly, quarterly, or annual schedule. Long-range planning can help you plan more effectively, and will allow time for creativity and consideration of special needs and events. See the Worship Worksheet on pages 8 and 9.

Be Excellent

God deserves your best in all you do. Strive for excellence—your best—in planning for worship as you allow God to guide you. Worship planning should always begin with prayer, seeking the Lord's direction and considering what your congregation needs on any given Sunday.

Identify Your Worship Leaders

Who plans the worship services in your church? Is it an individual effort or a team effort? Seek ways to incorporate those persons having regular responsibility for major portions of the worship service in the worship planning process. To begin, this should include the pastor, the music leader, and accompanists. If you wish to move gradually to a Worship Committee, add one or two members from the congregation, and other persons as necessary, for broad-based input. It is important, however, to keep focused on the objective: the worship of God.

Themes for Worship

While it's not always necessary (or even practical) to have thematic worship services, services which are developed around a specific theme seem to have a certain cohesiveness and clarity. Both of these factors are important for the congregation. Anything worship leaders can do to help worshipers connect with the purpose and intent of the service (have an encounter with the Lord, provide expressions of praise, allow for quiet introspection, extend opportunities for responding, and so forth) should be identified and enhanced.

The number of potential worship themes is limited only by your creativity to identify themes and develop meaningful services around them. Most hymnals provide a Thematic or Topical Index which groups hymns around related topics or themes. The following list represents only some of the many possibilities.

Advent
Ascension of Christ
Assurance
Atonement
Baptism
Benevolence
Bible
Blood of Christ
Children's Day
Christ the King
Christian Home Emphasis
Christian Warfare
Christmas
Church
Church Anniversary
Citizenship
Comfort
Commitment
Confession
Courage
Creation
Cross of Christ
Deacon Installation
Dedication
Discipleship
Easter
Education
Encouragement
Eternal Life
Evangelism
Faith and Trust
Family
Father's Day
Fellowship

Foreign Missions
Forgiveness
Founder's Day
Freedom
God the Father
Grace
Grandparents' Day
Heaven
Holiness and Purity
Holy Spirit
Home Missions
Homelessness
Hope
Independence Day
Invitation
Jesus the Son
Joy
Labor Day
Long-suffering
Lord's Supper
Lordship of Christ
Love
Memorial Day
Men's Day
Mercy
Ministry
Mother's Day
Music
Name of Christ
Nativity
Nature
New Year's
Ordination
Palm Sunday

Parent/Child Dedication
Patriotism
Peace
Pentecost
Praise and Adoration
Prayer
Providence
Redemption
Religious Liberty
Repentance
Resurrection
Return of Christ
Salvation
Security of the Believer
Senior Adult Day
Servanthood
Sin
Social Responsibility
Stewardship
Temptation
Testimony
Thanksgiving
Trinity
Trust
Victory
Vocation
Witness
Women's Day
Worker Recognition
World Hunger
Worship
Youth

How to Use the Worship Worksheet

The Worship Worksheet on pages 8 and 9 is designed to give you a place to gather ideas and suggestions for future worship services; it is not intended for use in planning next Sunday's service. To get the most from this worksheet, consider these suggestions.

1. Copy both sides of the worksheet onto one sheet of paper. Many copy machines are equipped with a "duplex" feature which can perform this process in one operation. Make 52 or 53 copies of the worksheet—one for each Sunday in a year. (You may want to duplicate 104 sheets if you intend to prepare a worksheet for Sunday evening services.)

2. Three-hole punch each sheet and place in a three-ring binder for convenience and ease of use.

3. Place a Sunday date on each sheet for an entire year.

4. Indicate on the worksheets, if possible, the emphasis or worship theme for each Sunday (for instance, all the holiday Sundays, special event Sundays, and so forth). Consult with your pastor and check denominational, state, associational, church, civil, school, and other calendars, as necessary, for additional information. Look at the list of worship themes found on page 6 for other ideas.

5. Begin to list hymn and other music possibilities, along with persons who may have music responsibilities in this service, as you begin the process of long-range planning for each service. NOTE: You won't plan the order of worship on this sheet; it's simply a place to gather ideas until you're ready to outline the order of service.

6. Notice that the worksheet has a place for medley and hymn treatment planning. Begin using the Medley Planning Sheet on page 14 and the Hymn Treatment Planning Sheet on page 11 to work out the details of these two items, then transfer that information to the Worship Worksheet.

7. Enlist soloists and other groups. Determine what they will sing. Plan choir music and list it.

8. List any special equipment needs you will have.

9. Use the information you've placed on the Worship Worksheet to outline the service two or three weeks prior to the service. Remember, it's easier to change from plans you've made than to have no plan at all.

10. Evaluate each service at the conclusion of that service. Did it go like you thought it would? If you had it to do over, what would you never do again, or what would you seriously modify? What was so effective that you will probably want to use it again? Make your evaluation precise, concise, and meaningful.

11. Remove the Worship Worksheet from the binder and place it in a file folder designated for that theme/emphasis. By doing this you will begin compiling a file on this theme for future reference. As you find other ideas from looking at church bulletins, talking with friends, reading books and magazines, or attending conferences, add these to your file. Replace the old worksheet by adding a new one to the end of the notebook, with the date and any information you have.

12. Share the contents of your notebook with the pastor on a regular basis. Encourage him to plan with you regularly.

Worship Worksheet

Date:_____ Service: _____ Theme/Emphasis: _____

Central Scripture Reference(s): _____

Notes/Ideas/Special Considerations: _____

_____

CONGREGATIONAL MUSIC ACTIVITIES

List potential hymns for this service and how they will be used (for example, traditional, call to worship, solo, instrumental, spoken, choir or other group, medley, invitation, and so forth). This list will likely contain more than you will use, but list several possibilities which could support the theme or emphasis.

No.	Title	Use

Choruses/Scripture Songs to Be Considered for Use in this Service:

Title	Source	*CCLI Item?

*CCLI—See "Hymn Medleys," page 12, paragraph seven.

Medley Planning:

Name of Hymn, Chorus, or Other Song	No.	Key	Modulation to Be Used

Hymn Treatment:

Title: _____

Stanza 1:_____

Stanza 2:_____

Stanza 3:_____

Stanza 4:_____

OTHER SERVICE MUSIC—CHORAL/VOCAL

Service Music to Be Used (Choir, Ensemble, or Other Singing Group):

Name of Group	Music Title

Soloists:

Name	Music Title

OTHER SERVICE MUSIC—INSTRUMENTAL

Instrumental Music to Be Used Including Piano and Organ:

Name	Instrument	Music Title	Use

AUDIO, VIDEO, SPECIAL EQUIPMENT, FURNISHINGS, MATERIALS NEEDED

Item	Quantity	Source	Date Requested

OTHER PLANNING ACTIONS REQUIRED FOR THIS SERVICE

EVALUATION

Hymn Treatments

Good hymn singing should be an exciting part of every worship service. Many of us have been part of a worship experience where the hymn singing was an incredible spiritual high. You may have attended church music conferences and workshops and heard the same kind of thrilling hymn singing. Experiences like these are hard to forget.

More often than not, hymns are sung in the more traditional manner, with the congregation singing one or more stanzas of each hymn. We've all heard jokes about how lonely the third stanza of a hymn must be, for it is often omitted.

An effective way to use hymns in worship services is to "treat" the hymn: that's another way of preparing or arranging the hymn for use by the congregation or the choir. Hymn treatments are often used as choir "specials" in many smaller membership churches. Because hymnals are found in most churches and choir members are familiar with the music, the hymnal is a good place to begin looking for choral music. You can make hymn treatments as simple or as involved as you wish. Remember, however, that the effectiveness is lost if the choir or congregation gets lost or confused about the instructions for singing the hymn. It's best to strive for noncomplicated treatments.

When planning a hymn treatment, study the nature of the hymn and the message of its text. Consider the resources you will need, whether from the choir, soloists, duets and other groups, or the congregation. Think also of the instrumentation available: piano, organ, and/or other instruments, and how and when they will be used. Consider whether or not the hymn will be "treated" entirely with music or whether some portion of it will be read or spoken. Use your own imagination and creativity when planning hymn treatments. Hymns may be treated singly or in combination with one or more hymns. Here are two examples:

Treatment I (single hymn)

Hymn 149 "Blessed Redeemer"

Introduction: Pianist plays bracketed introduction; Choir sings chorus to the end with piano accompaniment.

Stanza 1: Congregation sings softly to chorus with piano and organ providing quiet accompaniment; *omit* chorus.

Stanza 2: Choir sings softly to chorus with piano accompaniment.

Stanza 3: Soloist sings softly to chorus, building in volume on the phrase "My tongue shall praise Him forevermore," with organ. Soloist, choir, and congregation join together singing the final chorus, with piano and organ building in volume to the word "tree," which is sustained; sing the next phrase, growing softer, sustaining the word "pleading." The last phrase is sung very softly, allowing the music to fade at the end.

Treatment II (two or more hymns)

Hymn 485 "Stand Up, Stand Up for Jesus" (B♭) **and Hymn 141 "The Old Rugged Cross"** (B♭)

Introduction: Organist plays bracketed introduction of Hymn 485.

Stanza 1: Choir, with piano and organ accompaniment

Stanza 2: Congregation with organ only

Stanza 3: Choir with piano only

Stanza 4: Choir and congregation, with piano and organ

Hymn 141 **"The Old Rugged Cross,"** chorus only, unaccompanied

Hymn Treatment Planning Sheet

DATE: _____

HYMN NO. _____ **HYMN TITLE:** _____

Introduction: _____

Stanza 1: _____

Stanza 2: _____

Stanza 3: _____

Stanza 4: _____

Stanza 5: _____

Notes: _____

_____

_____

_____

_____

_____

_____

DATE: _____

HYMN NO. _____ **HYMN TITLE:** _____

Introduction: _____

Stanza 1: _____

Stanza 2: _____

Stanza 3: _____

Stanza 4: _____

Stanza 5: _____

Notes: _____

_____

_____

_____

_____

_____

_____

Hymn Medleys

Creating and singing hymn medleys as part of congregational worship is one hymn-singing technique which has the potential for creating an exciting new dimension in what may otherwise be sleepy congregational singing. A medley is simply a linking of two or more hymns and/or choruses into a cohesive musical unit. Many medleys require about the same amount of time to sing as a four-stanza hymn, although some may be longer or shorter. Each hymn or chorus in a medley may be related thematically or topically, may be related by key, or in other ways. Several types of modulation are available for moving smoothly from key to key in a medley. Modulation techniques are discussed later in this book.

Medleys can be used effectively in a number of ways in the church. If your choir sings much of its music from the hymnal, consider creating hymn medleys for greater interest and variety. In addition to Sunday morning and evening worship services, medleys are useful in revival services, crusades, camps, and retreats where printed music and hymnals may not be available. Several hymnals provide ready-to-sing medleys, including *The Baptist Hymnal*, 1991, and *The Christian Praise Hymnal*, both of which have 28 medleys.

To create a medley, first select a theme or topic. Select several hymns and choruses (more than you will need) which relate to the theme, then narrow the list. A good medley should provide an interesting arrangement of keys and contrast in mood and tempo; medleys may be sung alternately by congregation, choir, soloist or ensemble, or played by the instrumentalists alone. Be careful not to ask the congregation to sing a medley that is too long. Longer medleys sung entirely by the congregation run the risk of tiring the singers and often prove to be too confusing to follow.

The second step in creating a medley is to determine the key of each hymn or chorus. Some hymnals give the key of each hymn in an index. The Modulation Chart on page 23 will also help you identify keys. It may be helpful to write the name of the key directly above the first line key signature of each hymn. This will allow you to see the key name at a glance when preparing medleys.

The third step is to determine the order in which the hymns and choruses will be sung. While any order is possible, the desire is to move from key to key in a pleasing manner, using modulations that are pleasant to the ear, and not awkward or too distant. Use the Modulation Chart found on page 23 for assistance in placing the contents of your medley in an order which allows for smooth key changes.

The next step of medley preparation is to determine how much of any one hymn or chorus to use. Answer these questions: How many different songs are in this medley? How much time will be required to sing it? Will it tire or confuse the congregation? Will the congregation be able to quickly turn from tune to tune in the hymnal, or would a medley insert in the worship folder or bulletin make the process easier? Remember, as with any congregational music activity, the song leader is there to encourage people to sing and to provide the materials they need for ease of participation. If you determine that something might discourage someone from singing, try to find an alternative way of doing it.

NOTE: If your church is not already a member of the Christian Copyright Licensing, Inc. group, call 1-800-234-2446 to obtain information about how to legally copy music, and/or text, for congregational use. This group gives you access to more than 1000 music publishers, a real plus when looking for variety and for useful worship music material.

Once you have determined the order of the medley, the next step is to select the method of modulation you wish to use. For those accompanists who have little or no experience modulating between keys, this can be a traumatic experience. But with patience and practice, the methods explained on pages 21-28 will help them learn this technique and do it with ease. The music director should schedule some time each week to work exclusively with the accompanists. The time you spend with them practicing your song-leading skills, determining hymn tempos, or rehearsing choral and other music, will pay big dividends in every worship service and choir rehearsal. Make it a weekly habit.

As indicated in the above paragraph, the next step is to thoroughly rehearse with your accompanists each medley you create. Agreement should be reached as to where the modulation note or sequence should occur between the various elements of the medley. As a general rule, if a hymn or chorus is written in $\frac{4}{4}$ time, beat 3 is usually a good place to add it; if the hymn or chorus is in $\frac{3}{4}$ time, add the modulation note or sequence to beat 1. Working with your accompanist will enable you to reach a consensus as to where the modulation would be most effective and useful. Regardless of where or when you rehearse your medley, the most important thing to remember is this: It is much better to rehearse privately than in front of the congregation during a worship service!

The next consideration is to decide who will sing or play each unit of the medley. You have many choices: congregation, choir, ensemble, soloist, men, women, instrumental player, or others. Will everything be sung, or would reading a stanza aloud or silently be more effective? Would a reading, poem, or Scripture selection be effective as a unit of the medley with an instrumental background? (Remember, if a nonmusical element is used as part of the medley, but it has a musical background, the same careful planning process is required for the order and the key sequence used.)

You are now ready to prepare the medley for inclusion in the worship folder or bulletin. Because space is often limited in most printed orders of worship, you might consider listing all hymn and/or chorus numbers on a single line, giving the medley a title of its own or using the title of the first piece in the medley as the title to be printed. If your congregation sings from an image projected on a screen, perhaps all you'll need to do is prepare slides or cels for use on the overhead, or purchase those which are commercially prepared.

Using medleys can add that "something special" to involve the congregation in a musical experience in worship. Preparing them can even be fun. Keep a file of each medley you prepare, since you may wish to use it later for another occasion or church. Use medleys whenever they can help you accomplish specific aims or desires in the worship experience. Don't use a medley in every service. You may find the novelty of the experience wearing thin with the congregation, whose natural tendency is to sing things in the "more normal way." The following pages contain numerous medleys which have proven effective in worship services. Add your own to this list and watch it grow. An example of how to chart a medley is given below.

Medley Theme: The Name of Jesus

NAME OF HYMN OR CHORUS	NO.	KEY	MODULATION TO BE USED
"Glorify Thy Name" (congregation)	249	B♭	Add A♭ to beat 1 of last measure
"There's Something About That Name" (soloist)	177	E♭	Add D♭ to beat 1 of last measure
"Take the Name of Jesus with You" (congregation)	576	A♭	No modulation; moving to same key
"He Keeps Me Singing" (chorus only) (congregation)	425	A♭	End of medley

Medley Planning Sheet

Use this sheet to create and plan medleys of hymns, choruses, or other music for use in worship services. Here are some questions to keep in mind when creating a medley:

1. What is the purpose of the medley?
2. Will the medley have a unifying theme?
3. How long will the medley be?
4. Will the medley be sung by the congregation alone, or in part with others?
5. What type of modulations will be used and who will do them?
6. How convenient will the medley be for the congregation? (Are the hymns widely spaced, sequential, and so forth?)
7. How convenient will it be for the accompanists?
8. What type of accompaniment will the medley require?

Medley Theme: _____

NAME OF HYMN OR CHORUS	NO.	KEY	MODULATION TO BE USED

Medley Theme: _____

NAME OF HYMN OR CHORUS	NO.	KEY	MODULATION TO BE USED

Medley Theme: _____

NAME OF HYMN OR CHORUS	NO.	KEY	MODULATION TO BE USED

Hymn Medley List

Now that you are more familiar with how to create a medley, let's look at some which have been created using hymns and choruses from *The Baptist Hymnal, 1991.* You may have already discovered and used several of the 28 medleys featured in this hymnal. (See the Medley Index on page 767.) These medleys are enhanced by the transition material found in the Organ and Piano Editions of *The Baptist Hymnal, 1991.*

The medleys listed below may be played directly from the hymnal without any other outside material. Some feature hymns and choruses in the same key, while others are in closely related keys. The medleys are related by theme or topic. For ease of singing by the congregation, these medleys are in exact or nearly exact numerical order. Use the Modulation Chart on page 23, or select the technique of your choice.

Topical Medleys

TOPIC	NO.	TITLE	KEY
Mercy	24	"He Is Able to Deliver Thee"	B♭
	25	"There's a Wideness in God's Mercy"	B♭
	22	"Bless His Holy Name"	E♭
	23	"God Is So Good"	E♭
Providence	67	"Come, Ye Disconsolate"	C
	68	"My Shepherd Will Supply My Need"	C
	69	"Eternal Father, Strong to Save"	C
Carols	85	"The First Nowell"	D
	87	"Joy to the World! The Lord Is Come"	D
	89	"O Come, All Ye Faithful"	G
Carols	86	"O Little Town of Bethlehem"	F
	88	"Hark! The Herald Angels Sing"	F
	90	"Carols Sing"	F
Carols	90	"Carols Sing"	F
	91	"Silent Night, Holy Night"	B♭
	93	"It Came upon the Midnight Clear"	B♭
	94	"Angels, from the Realms of Glory"	B♭
Carols	96	"Good Christian Men, Rejoice"	F
	97	"Sing Hosannas"	F
	100	"Angels We Have Heard on High"	F
Carols	109	"Love Came Down at Christmas"	F
	110	"That Boy-Child of Mary"	F
	112	"He Is Born"	F
Savior and Lord	175	" 'Man of Sorrows,' What a Name"	B♭
	176	"Fairest Lord Jesus"	E♭
	177	"There's Something About That Name"	E♭
Friend	180	"Jesus, Lover of My Soul"	F
	181	"No, Not One"	F
	182	"What a Friend We Have in Jesus"	F
Return	195	"What If It Were Today"	C
	196	"We Shall Behold Him"	C
	197	"Rejoice, the Lord Is King"	C

TOPIC	NO.	TITLE	KEY
Name	205	"Jesus Is the Sweetest Name I Know"	C
	203	"His Name Is Wonderful"	F
	204	"Glorious Is Thy Name"	F
Praise	211	"I Love Thee"	E♭
	212	"I Love You, Lord"	E♭
	214	"Sing Hallelujah to the Lord"	E♭
Praise	225	"Jesus, the Very Thought of Thee"	G
	226	"O Praise the Gracious Power"	G
	227	"Praise Him! Praise Him!"	G
Trinity	246	"The Love of God	Scripture
	247	"Come, Thou Almighty King"	F
	248	"God, Our Father, We Adore Thee"	B♭
	249	"Glorify Thy Name"	B♭
Submission	280	"Jesus, Keep Me Near the Cross"	F
	281	"Speak to My Heart"	F
	282	"Living for Jesus"	F
Submission	287	"Take My Life, Lead Me, Lord"	D♭
	289	"My Lord, I Did Not Choose You"	D♭
	291	"Beneath the Cross of Jesus"	D♭
Invitation	307	"Just As I Am"	E♭
	308	"Pass Me Not, O Gentle Savior"	A♭
	309	"Lord, I'm Coming Home"	A♭
	310	"Out of My Bondage, Sorrow, and Night"	A♭
	311	"Let Jesus Come into Your Heart"	A♭
Invitation	308	"Pass Me Not, O Gentle Savior"	A♭
	309	"Lord, I'm Coming Home"	A♭
	310	"Out of My Bondage, Sorrow, and Night"	A♭
	311	"Let Jesus Come into Your Heart"	A♭
Invitation	312	"Softly and Tenderly"	G
	315	"Room at the Cross"	G
	317	"Only Trust Him"	G
	316	"Jesus Is Tenderly Calling"	C
Invitation	322	"Ye Must Be Born Again"	E♭
	324	"Have You Been to Calvary"	E♭
	325	"Whiter than Snow"	A♭
Grace	329	"Grace Greater than Our Sin"	G
	330	"Amazing Grace! How Sweet the Sound"	G
	328	"Wonderful Grace of Jesus"	C
Assurance	334	"Blessed Assurance, Jesus Is Mine"	D
	336	"I Am His, and He Is Mine"	D
	337	"I Know Whom I Have Believed"	D
Grace	339	"Not What My Hands Have Done"	D
	340	"He Hideth My Soul"	D
	341	"Forgiven"	G

TOPIC	NO.	TITLE	KEY
Assurance	344	"Jesus Loves Me"	D
	346	"He's Got the Whole World in His Hands"	D
	345	"Now I Belong to Jesus"	G
Lord's Supper	366	"Let Us Break Bread Together"	E♭
	368	"Here, at Your Table, Lord"	E♭
	370	"This Is a Day of New Beginnings"	E♭
Family of God	386	"The Family of God"	F
	387	"Blest Be the Tie"	F
	384	"The Bond of Love"	B♭
Faith	409	"O the Deep, Deep Love of Jesus"	A♭
	412	"My Faith Has Found a Resting Place"	A♭
	410	"It Is Well with My Soul"	D♭
Trust	417	"Trusting Jesus"	G
	418	"I've Got Peace Like a River"	G
	420	"I Will Trust in the Lord"	G
Triumph	428	"Ring the Bells of Heaven"	B♭
	429	"All That Thrills My Soul"	B♭
	431	"There's a Glad New Song"	B♭
Joy	437	"Greater Is He That Is in Me"	F
	438	"Heaven Came Down"	F
	439	"O Happy Day That Fixed My Choice"	F
	440	"In the Presence of the Lord"	F
Prayer	445	"Sweet Hour of Prayer"	C
	446	"Take Time to Be Holy"	F
	447	"Trust and Obey"	F
	448	"Just a Closer Walk with Thee"	B♭
Prayer	451	"Tell It to Jesus"	G
	452	"He Is So Precious to Me"	G
	453	"How Sweet the Name of Jesus Sounds"	G
Prayer	454	"God, Our Father, You Have Led Us"	E♭
	455	"I Must Tell Jesus"	E♭
	456	"Precious Lord, Take My Hand"	A♭
Home	508	"Lord, for the Gift of Children"	E♭
	510	"O Lord, May Church and Home Combine"	E♭
	509	"Your Love, O God, Has Called Us Here"	A♭
Testimony	537	"I Will Sing the Wondrous Story"	E♭
	539	"Satisfied"	E♭
	541	"Why Do I Sing About Jesus"	A♭
Evangelism	557	"People Need the Lord"	C
	561	"One by One"	F
	559	"Rescue the Perishing"	B♭

TOPIC	NO.	TITLE	KEY
Evangelism	575	"I Will Sing of My Redeemer"	A♭
	576	"Take the Name of Jesus with You"	A♭
	577	"The Old Ship of Zion"	A♭
Evangelism	584	"We Have Heard the Joyful Sound"	D
	581	"We Have Heard the Joyful Sound"	G
	582	"Send Me, O Lord, Send Me"	G
Stewardship	614	"Fill the Earth with Music"	E♭
	615	"To the Work"	E♭
	616	"Trust, Try, and Prove Me"	E♭
Patriotic	634	"My Country, 'Tis of Thee"	F
	633	"Mine Eyes Have Seen the Glory"	B♭
	630	"America the Beautiful"	B♭
	629	"God of our Fathers"	E♭
Thanksgiving	637	"Come, Ye Thankful People, Come"	F
	638	"Now Thank We All Our God"	F
	639	"As Men of Old Their First Fruits Brought"	F
	640	"Let All Things Now Living"	F

More Medleys

The medleys listed in this section are created from hymns and choruses throughout the hymnal. They are related thematically and topically, may be widely scattered throughout the hymnal, and may require one or several modulation techniques. Note: some medleys may not require a modulation between every song even though there is a key change. Medleys which require no modulation between certain songs are indicated in the list below with an asterisk (*). In those cases, simply begin playing the next song. The medleys vary in length. For those which contain more than four titles, consider using a variety of music resources for singing them in a worship service. For instance, a longer medley may be sung by congregation, choir, soloist, ensemble, or played by an instrumentalist. This practice does not tire the congregation and gives them time to find the next song of the medley. For convenience, prepare a bulletin insert with the words only or with words and music. Or, you may wish to list the medley on a single line in the bulletin. For example, Cross of Christ Medley (for a title) with the numbers of the medley components in this manner: 138, 280, 141, 139, 140. This saves bulletin or worship folder space, which typically is limited.

TOPIC	NO.	TITLE	KEY
God's Greatness	12	"Great Is the Lord"	C
	29	"How Majestic Is Your Name"	C
	82	"Emmanuel"	C
Cross of Christ	138	"At Calvary"	C
	280	"Jesus, Keep Me Near the Cross"	F
	141	"The Old Rugged Cross"	B♭
	139	"At the Cross"	E♭
	140	"Down at the Cross"	A♭

TOPIC	NO.	TITLE	KEY
God's Love and Grace	147	"And Can It Be"	G
	185	"Jesus! What a Friend for Sinners"	G
	329	"Grace Greater than Our Sin"	G
Thankfulness	153	"My Tribute"	B♭
	10	"How Great Thou Art"	B♭
God's Love	547	"I Stand Amazed in the Presence"	A♭
	146	"O How He Loves You and Me"	A♭
	579	"Shine, Jesus, Shine"	A♭
Name of Jesus	202	"All Hail the Power of Jesus' Name"	G
	236	"Bless That Wonderful Name"	G
	205	"Jesus Is the Sweetest Name I Know"	C
	198	"At the Name of Jesus"	F
	207	"Name of All Majesty"	B♭
Name of Jesus	205	"Jesus Is the Sweetest Name I Know"	C
	82	"Emmanuel"	C
	203	"His Name Is Wonderful"	F*
	236	"Bless That Wonderful Name"	G
Majesty and Power	215	"Majesty"	B♭
	10	"How Great Thou Art"	B♭
	22	"Bless His Holy Name"	E♭
Name of Jesus	217	"Oh, How I Love Jesus"	A♭
	206	"Blessed Be the Name"	A♭*
	203	"His Name Is Wonderful"	F
	204	"Glorious Is Thy Name"	F
	249	"Glorify Thy Name"	B♭
	177	"There's Something About That Name"	E♭
	576	"Take the Name of Jesus with You"	A♭
	425	"He Keeps Me Singing" (Chorus only)	A♭
Praise and Adoration	224	"Holy Ground"	E♭
	177	"There's Something About That Name"	E♭
	212	"I Love You, Lord"	E♭
Conviction/Submission	244	"Spirit of the Living God"	F
	281	"Speak to My Heart"	F
	280	"Jesus, Keep Me Near the Cross"	F
Adoration	256	"Father, I Adore You"	F
	203	"His Name Is Wonderful"	F
	3	"Worthy of Worship"	F
Joy	443	"This Joy That I Have"	F*
	192	"Soon and Very Soon"	G
	236	"Bless That Wonderful Name"	G
Walk with Jesus	448	"Just a Closer Walk with Thee"	B♭
	279	"O Master, Let Me Walk with Thee"	E♭*
	465	"I Want Jesus to Walk with Me"	Cm

TOPIC	NO.	TITLE	KEY
Commitment	486	"Lord, Here Am I"	C
	569	"Make Me a Blessing" (chorus only)	C
Missions	591	"Hark, the Voice of Jesus Calling" (use this text, but play 471 in key of G)	G
	486	"Lord, Here Am I"	C
	657	"Go Out and Tell"	C

Hymn Strings in Same Key or Closely Related Keys

Look on page xiii of *The Baptist Hymnal, 1991*, or *The Christian Praise Hymnal*. This is the Contents page. Under the heading "The Hymns," you will notice there are four grand divisions of hymns and related worship aids: "The Glory of God," "The Love of God," "The People of God," and "The Witness of the People of God." Within each of these grand divisions are subdivisions which contain smaller groupings of hymns on closely related subjects.

As you look through any of these divisions or subdivisions, you will notice many instances of topically related hymns in the same key or closely related keys, often in exact or approximate numerical order. These hymn groupings are good sources for medleys. Here is a listing of several groupings which could be used as medleys. Each listing below may be used as a medley. When key changes are required, refer to the modulation techniques described later in this book.

NO.	TITLE	KEY	NO.	TITLE	KEY
22	"Bless His Holy Name"	E♭	205	"Jesus Is the Sweetest Name I Know"	C
23	"God Is So Good"	E♭	203	"His Name Is Wonderful"	F
			204	"Glorious Is Thy Name"	F
45	"Everything Was Made by God"	D			
46	"All Things Bright and Beautiful"	D	211	"I Love Thee"	E♭
			212	"I Love You, Lord"	E♭
70	"How Great Our God's Majestic Name"	D	214	"Sing Hallelujah to the Lord"	E♭
71	"On Eagle's Wings"	D			
			222	"I've Come to Tell"	G
145	"Alas, and Did My Savior Bleed"	A♭	223	"Alleluia"	G
146	"O How He Loves You and Me"	A♭			
			247	"Come, Thou Almighty King"	F
154	"A Purple Robe"	D	248	"God, Our Father, We Adore Thee"	B♭
155	"I Know a Fount"	D	249	"Glorify Thy Name"	B♭
157	"Worthy Is the Lamb"	G			
			270	"No, Not Despairingly"	E♭
176	"Fairest Lord Jesus"	E♭	273	"Freely, Freely"	E♭
177	"There's Something About That Name"	E♭			
			340	"He Hideth My Soul"	D
185	"Jesus! What a Friend for Sinners"	G	341	"Forgiven"	G
186	"Walking Along with Jesus"	C			
			344	"Jesus Loves Me"	D
189	"The Lily of the Valley"	F	346	"He's Got the Whole World in His Hands"	D
190	"Jesus, My Friend, Is Great"	F			
			378	"Christian Hearts, in Love United"	G
			380	"In the Family of God"	G

Some Things You Wanted to Know About Modulating*
*BUT WERE AFRAID TO ASK

"Modulation" is a frightening word to many accompanists, and even more frightening to those music leaders who often must depend on their accompanists for the knowledge and skill to do such things. It doesn't have to be a frightening or nerve-racking experience, complete with sweaty palms, memory lapses, and near trauma. When looked at closely, both the music leader and accompanist can discover ways to move smoothly from key to key with little or no effort. This chapter will lead you through several modulation techniques. With a bit of practice each week, you'll soon discover how little effort it really takes to modulate.

Modulation, simply defined, is a shift to another key. There are many routes which can be taken to get to a new key; some are easy, and some are quite involved. Your own keyboard skills and ability will determine which route you choose, but you can do it. These techniques have been collected for ease of use and application to congregational music activities. Of course, they may also be used in any application.

For further study, contact your associational music director or state music department and ask when the next workshop for church accompanists will be held. Many states and associations offer workshops for both experienced and inexperienced accompanists. If you let them know exactly where you need help, perhaps a workshop session could be designed specifically on how to modulate. In the meantime, let's see if these techniques will help.

Modulation Technique 1

This is perhaps the easiest technique of all. It has been referred to as the fail-safe method of modulating. It utilizes the leading power of the V (dominant) or V^7 (dominant seventh) to I (tonic) chord relationship. Practically every piece of music, and certainly most hymns, end with these two chords. Playing these chords immediately places you in the key of the hymn you are about to play.

Suppose you are playing "To God Be the Glory" (No. 4), which is in the key of A♭. The next hymn in the service is "Glorious Is Thy Name" (No. 204), in the key of F. You do not want a break or pause in the music, but want to move into the new key and begin an introduction. Using this technique, finish playing "To God Be the Glory," then immediately play the final two chords of "Glorious Is Thy Name." You have quickly established the new key, and now have a choice to either begin singing immediately, or move into an introduction. See this illustrated in Examples 1 and 2 on page 22.

EXAMPLE 1

EXAMPLE 2

Modulation Technique 2

This technique of modulating is based on the music theory principle of the **Circle of Fifths.** Wait! Don't panic! It's not often I mention the word "theory" in writing or in casual conversation, but an understanding of its basic premise will help you to better understand how this technique works.

The Circle of Fifths is an arrangement of all 12 pitch names in a closed circle. These pitches are arranged in such a way as to be a perfect fifth (five note names arranged in a whole step, whole step, half step, whole step grouping). For example, beginning with C, count up five notes (including C) and you arrive at G, the next key in the Circle of Fifths. Five notes up from G is D, and so forth. Each time you move around the circle you add one sharp ($\sharp$) or ($\flat$) as the case may be. Here's what the Circle of Fifths looks like:

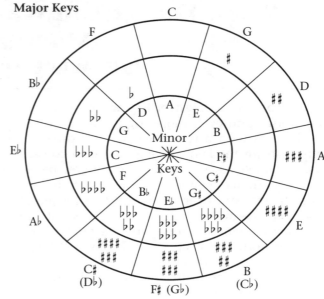

While the Circle of Fifths is useful, it may not always be easily understood by those with little or no formal music training; in fact, it may resemble something very sinister to some people. But it's actually quite user friendly. This particular technique is very useful when planning medleys.

For the application of the Circle of Fifths as a modulation technique, let's rearrange the circle into a chart which, hopefully, will be more easily understood. It follows on page 23. But first, a few simple steps.

Step 1: In the chart which follows, use the information in columns one and two to identify the key of the hymn or chorus. It may be helpful to write the key name on the hymn page for future reference.

Step 2: Just before ending the first hymn or chorus, prepare to add the modulation note in column three to the appropriate beat of the last measure or to the final chord. The addition of the modulation note to the final chord creates the V^7 chord of the next key in the chart.

Step 3: Repeat steps 1 and 2 as often as necessary. Note: If two hymns appear in succession in a medley in the same key, do not add the modulation note; add this note only when you are ready to change keys.

Step 4: Always move from left to right and top to bottom through the modulation chart; never move from bottom to top or right to left. Use other techniques for these types of modulations.

Step 5: Do not skip a line between modulations. For example, if one hymn is in the key of F and the next in the medley is in the key of E$\flat$, play through the sequence in the chart, or use another modulation technique.

Step 6: The last line of the chart moves naturally back to the first line to continue the process.

Modulation Chart

IF BEGINNING KEY SIGNATURE HAS...	THE KEY USUALLY IS...	ADD THIS NOTE TO FINAL CHORD TO MODULATE TO NEXT KEY
5♯	B	A
4♯	E	D
3♯	A	G
2♯	D	C
1♯	G	F
0♯ or 0♭	C	B♭
1♭	F	E♭
2♭	B♭	A♭
3♭	E♭	D♭
4♭	A♭	G♭
5♭	D♭	C♭ (B on piano)
6♭	G♭	F♭ (E on piano)

Note: Modulations occurring after last line in chart (6♭) move automatically back to top of chart to continue or repeat the process.

Modulation Technique 3

If you desire to have a somewhat fuller-sounding modulation between songs, you may wish to refer to the modulation chart on pages 24-25. This chart, also available in the Organ and Piano Editions of *The Baptist Hymnal,* 1991, and *The Christian Praise Hymnal*, enables you to modulate from one key to another by playing a series of chords, usually not more than 12. The instructions for reading this chart are as follows:

1. Select the old key (the key of the song played first) from the column at the left. Depending on the rhythm of the final measure of the first song, you may elect to play the measure as is, or to play it in the rhythm compatible with the previous key.

2. Next, move horizontally across the chart on the same line and stop at the measure under the new key column.

3. Play the measure from step two, then move to the bottom of that column and play the measure found there. This measure will provide the cadence that will establish the new key. You are now ready to begin playing the next song in the new key. In other words:

A. select old key from left column;
B. play measure on same line under new key;
C. play measure at bottom of page.

There are some general considerations which will make the use of this chart even more effective. Because styles of music vary so widely, you may find that some of the chords and cadences are too different in style, voicing, octave, and harmonic structure. Use your own judgment as to whether or not the progressions in the chart will be useful and compatible.

A second consideration concerns reading the chart itself. You will probably discover that it's almost impossible for the eye to locate and follow the two or three measures for each modulation in the chart. Here's a suggestion: Make a copy of the measures you need for each modulation; highlight those measures you will use, or cut and affix them near the spot on the music where the modulation will occur. Because you will refer to this chart often, it will be impractical to mark or cut the original chart itself. *(See chart on pages 24 and 25.)*

Other Modulation Techniques

Sometimes it's helpful to have a collection of models showing how something is done. That's what you'll find in this section. Examples A-N show how to modulate up or down by whole and half steps, and illustrate several other helpful techniques. They are useful in a variety of situations, with suggestions provided with each musical illustration.

The final stanza of a hymn is an effective place for a modulation to occur. Just prior to singing the last stanza, modulate a half step up from the original key. Examples A and B illustrate how this can be done. Many accompanists can think in the new key. If your accompanist has never tried this, remember: the harmonic and chord structure does not change, and hand positions remain the same. If this proves too difficult to do, you might try to find the same music

in different keys. Check other hymnals or songbooks.

Look for a common tone between the last chord of the current song and the pivot chord which enables you to move smoothly into the new key. The common tone will be the same note name common to both these chords, hence the name. Play the common tone on top of the right-hand chord prior to leaving the current key. Keep the common tone in the same position (on top) of the pivot chord so the relationship between the current and the new key is easy to hear. For smoother voice leading, move to the other notes of the following chord by small intervals, as illustrated in the examples.

(Examples A-N © 1994 CCM Communications. From *Worship Leader*, Vol. 3, No. 3, May/June 1994, 15. Used by permission.)

MODULATING UP BY HALF STEPS

(Useful when modulating on final stanza of hymn, or for choir warm-ups.)

EXAMPLE A

EXAMPLE B

EXPLANATION: The old tonic or key note becomes the 3rd of the new V^7 chord, which is also the leading tone of the new key. The left hand can move downward two whole steps to find the root of the new V^7 chord, which then resolves to a new tonic a half step above the old key.

MODULATING DOWN BY HALF STEPS

(Useful for choir vocal exercises or when you desire to musically move the congregation from an emotional peak in the service to a less intense portion of the worship experience.)

EXAMPLE C

EXAMPLE D

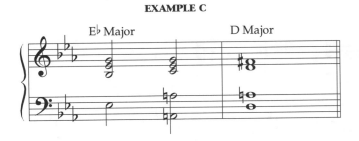

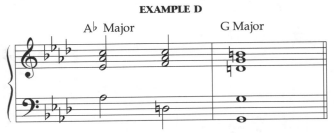

EXPLANATION: The root and the third of the old tonic are kept as common tones. These two notes then become the fifth and seventh of the diminished V^7 chord in the new key.

MODULATING UP BY WHOLE STEPS

EXPLANATION: The fifth of the old tonic chord becomes the seventh of the new V^7 chord.

MODULATING DOWN BY WHOLE STEPS

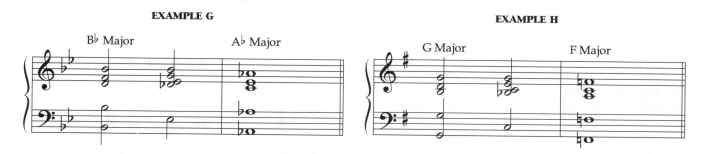

EXPLANATION: The tonic of the old key becomes the fifth of the new V^7 chord.

MODULATING THROUGH THE FLAT KEYS
(Enables you to modulate up a perfect fourth or down a perfect fifth.)

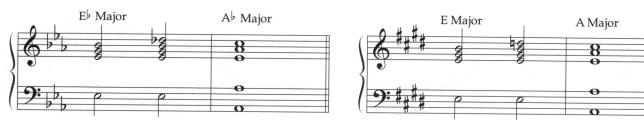

EXPLANATION: Adding a flat to the key signature or subtracting a sharp enables you to modulate up a perfect fourth or down a perfect fifth. Add a minor seventh to the old tonic chord and it becomes the V^7 chord of the new key. (Note: This is the method utilized in the modulation chart discussed earlier.)

MODULATING THROUGH THE SHARP KEYS

(Enables you to modulate up a perfect fifth or down a perfect fourth.)

EXAMPLE K

EXAMPLE L

EXPLANATION: Adding a sharp to the key signature or subtracting a flat enables you to modulate up a perfect fifth or down a perfect fourth. Keep the old tonic note as a common tone on top of the chord. It then becomes the seventh of the new V^7 chord.

In general, when using common tone modulations to any key,
look for a common tone between the old tonic chord and . . .
- the I or tonic chord of the new key, or
- the V or dominant chord of the new key, or
- the IV or subdominant chord of the new key.

EXAMPLE M

The new key should be established firmly in any modulation. The strongest chord progression in the new key for establishing this is:
- the new tonic chord in second inversion or I $^6_4$ position, with the fifth of the chord in the bass, followed by
- the V^7 chord, followed by
- the new tonic chord in its root position, with the root of the chord in the bass. See Example M.

EXAMPLE N

Use the chord progressions in Example N for practice in becoming familiar with all keys:

I   VI   III   IV   II   I $^6_4$ V^7 I

Modulations are transitions, or bridges, which enable smooth passage from one key to the next. Effective modulations can give a worship service a "polished" or well-planned feeling on the part of the congregation and music leaders alike. They can be used to prevent that "start and stop" feeling between hymns or other music units of a worship service.

Both music leader and accompanists are encouraged to practice modulation techniques until they become a natural part of your directing or accompanying style. The faster you develop this technique, the more quickly you can incorporate them into the various music activities of your church and music ministry.

Hymns by Category

Throughout the hymnal, there are hymns and choruses which may be grouped into more specialized categories than may appear in the Topical Index of the hymnal. For instance, because of space limitations, there is no separate listing of all the choruses in the hymnal. The specialized lists which follow group these hymns and choruses by type or style. This kind of grouping allows for faster access to the particular music you may need.

If, for example, you wish to plan a service on world missions, you may consult the "Hymns of Ethnic Origin" list for hymns and choruses from a specific country. (Consult the *Handbook to The Baptist Hymnal* for more detailed information.) Another list provides hymns in unison for choirs with limited part-singing experience. Consult the lists which follow whenever you need a specialized hymn or chorus for a specific use.

Choruses

NO.	TITLE	KEY	NO.	TITLE	KEY
463	"All Day Long"	F	222	"I've Come to Tell"	G
223	"Alleluia"	G	418	"I've Got Peace Like a River"	G
233	"Behold the Lamb"	E♭	205	"Jesus Is the Sweetest Name I Know"	C
22	"Bless His Holy Name"	E♭	592	"Jesus Loves the Little Children"	A♭
236	"Bless That Wonderful Name"	G	234	"King of Kings"	Gm
479	"Children of God"	D	560	"Lead Me to Some Soul Today"	G
313	"Come, Let Us Reason"	D	220	"Lift Him Up"	G
82	"Emmanuel"	C	457	"Lord, Be Glorified"	D
45	"Everything Was Made by God"	D	215	"Majesty"	B♭
256	"Father, I Adore You"	F	146	"O How He Loves You and Me"	A♭
250	"Father, Son, Holy Spirit"	C	228	"Oh, How Good Is Christ the Lord"	D
427	"For He Alone Is Worthy"	G	71	"On Eagle's Wings"	D
341	"Forgiven"	G	561	"One by One"	F
273	"Freely, Freely"	E♭	534	"Only Believe"	D♭
249	"Glorify Thy Name"	B♭	499	"Open Our Eyes, Lord"	D
23	"God Is So Good"	E♭	557	"People Need the Lord"	C
437	"Greater Is He That Is in Me"	F	31	"Praise Him, All Ye Little Children"	E♭
12	"Great Is the Lord"	C	433	"Rejoice in the Lord Always"	F
178	"He Is Lord"	G	478	"Seek Ye First"	E♭
203	"His Name Is Wonderful"	F	214	"Sing Hallelujah to the Lord"	Cm
224	"Holy Ground"	E♭	192	"Soon and Very Soon"	G
254	"Holy, Holy"	C	244	"Spirit of the Living God"	F
343	"Holy Is His Name"	F	384	"The Bond of Love"	B♭
9	"Holy Is the Lord"	G	386	"The Family of God"	F
666	"Holy Is the Lord"	E♭	194	"The King Is Coming"	A
622	"Holy Lord"	F	37	"The Majesty and Glory of Your Name"	C
230	"How I Love You"	C	593	"The Whole World Is Singing"	D
29	"How Majestic Is Your Name"	C	536	"There Is a Savior"	D♭
155	"I Know a Fount"	D	177	"There's Something About That Name"	E♭
212	"I Love You, Lord"	E♭	359	"This Is the Day"	E♭
420	"I Will Trust in the Lord"	G	443	"This Joy That I Have"	F
488	"I'm Just a Child"	C	474	"We Are Climbing Jacob's Ladder"	D
53	"In His Time"	D	361	"We Have Come into His House"	E♭
380	"In the Family of God"	G	213	"We Will Glorify"	D
174	"In the Name of the Lord"	G	610	"What Can I Give Him"	B♭
440	"In the Presence of the Lord"	F	460	"When I Pray"	D

Hymns of Ethnic Origin

This list contains hymns whose text and/or music has an ethnic origin, background, or influence. They are especially useful during foreign missions services or when emphasizing the culture, music, and traditions of other nations and peoples. You may wish to share this list with missions leaders in your church for consideration when planning services, studies, or other events.

NUMBER	KEY	TITLE	ORIGIN
105	C	"Child in the Manger"	Gaelic
55	D	"Children of the Heavenly Father"	Sweden
167	E minor	"Christ Is Risen"	Argentina
66	E♭	"Day by Day"	Sweden
459	D	"Dear Lord, Lead Me Day by Day"	Philippine
112	F	"He Is Born"	France
179	C dorian	"Here, O Lord, Your Servants Gather"	Japan
108	C	"How Great Our Joy"	Germany
305	D♭	"I Have Decided to Follow Jesus"	India
222	G	"I've Come to Tell"	Cuba
106	G	"Infant Holy, Infant Lowly"	Poland
501	D	"Jesu, Jesu, Fill Us with Your Love"	Ghana
477	F	"Jesus' Hands Were Kind Hands"	France
190	F	"Jesus, My Friend, Is Great"	Japan
234	G minor	"King of Kings"	Hebrew
508	E♭	"Lord, for the Gift of Children"	Finland
49	C minor	"Many and Great, O God"	American Indian
48	C	"Morning Has Broken"	Gaelic
412	E♭	"My Faith Has Found a Resting Place"	Norway
38	D minor	"O Sing a Song to God"	Spain
107	D	"Oh, Come, Little Children"	Germany
228	D	"Oh, How Good Is Christ the Lord"	Puerto Rico
645	F	"Praise and Thanksgiving"	Alsatian
97	F	"Sing Hosannas"	Poland
111	E minor	"Sing We Now of Christmas"	France
110	F	"That Boy-Child of Mary"	Malawi
34	E minor	"The God of Abraham Praise"	Hebrew
127	E minor	"The King of Glory Comes"	Israeli
497	G	"The Master Hath Come"	Welsh
613	F	"The Servant Song"	New Zealand
186	C	"Walking Along with Jesus"	Cuba
636	D	"We Gather Together"	Holland

Hymns of African-American Tradition or Origin

The hymns in the following list are of African-American origin, with text and/or music written by Black authors and composers. It contains both traditional Negro Spirituals and songs by more contemporary writers. They are useful in services emphasizing race relations, missions, spirituals, and so forth, and may be sung by the congregation, choir, ensemble, soloists, or others.

NO.	TITLE	KEY	NO.	TITLE	KEY
463	"All Day Long"	F	366	"Let Us Break Bread Together"	E♭
22	"Bless His Holy Name"	E♭	627	"Lift Every Voice and Sing"	A♭
236	"Bless That Wonderful Name"	G	489	"Lord, I Want to Be a Christian"	E♭
479	"Children of God"	D	153	"My Tribute"	B♭
346	"He's Got the Whole World in His Hands"	D	192	"Soon and Very Soon"	G
465	"I Want Jesus to Walk with Me"	Cm	133	"The Blood Will Never Lose Its Power"	A♭
420	"I Will Trust in the Lord"	G	577	"The Old Ship of Zion"	A♭
432	"It's So Wonderful"	G	269	"There Is a Balm in Gilead"	F
418	"I've Got Peace Like a River"	G	443	"This Joy That I Have"	F
501	"Jesu, Jesu, Fill Us with Your Love"	D	474	"We Are Climbing Jacob's Ladder"	D
319	"Jesus Calls You Now"	D	156	"Were You There"	E♭
448	"Just a Closer Walk with Thee"	B♭			

Hymns Written in Unison (All or Part)

Many churches often have two adult choirs: the group that comes to weekly rehearsal, and the group that comes to Sunday morning service. Occasionally the two groups meet on Sunday and the choir loft is full. It's when these two groups don't get together on Sunday that every choir director needs a handy list of easy-to-learn, ready-to-sing music. This list, for the most part, contains hymns which are all, or nearly all, in unison. A good, strong unison sound can make even a small choir sound big. Refer to this list when you need a "Plan B" fast! These hymns are also strong congregational songs, and may be useful as solos.

NO.	TITLE	KEY	NO.	TITLE	KEY
12	"Great Is the Lord"	C	171	"Sound Aloud the Trumpet"	G
27	"All Creatures of Our God and King"	E♭	174	"In the Name of the Lord"	G
28	"Let All the World in Every Corner Sing"	D	179	"Here, O Lord, Your Servants Gather"	Cd
32	"Praise, My Soul, the King of Heaven"	D	186	"Walking Along with Jesus"	C
38	"O Sing a Song to God"	Dm	190	"Jesus, My Friend, Is Great"	F
45	"Everything Was Made by God"	D	214	"Sing Hallelujah to the Lord"	Cm
48	"Morning Has Broken"	C	222	"I've Come to Tell"	G
60	"Be Thou My Vision"	E♭	229	"All Praise to Thee"	F
71	"On Eagle's Wings"	D	234	"King of Kings"	Gm
80	"Let All Mortal Flesh Keep Silence"	Dm	240	"Spirit, Now Live in Me"	C
81	"Tell Out, My Soul, the Greatness"	D	251	"Of the Father's Love Begotten"	E♭
82	"Emmanuel"	C	303	"Just As I Am"	E♭
105	"Child in the Manger"	C	346	"He's Got the Whole World in His Hands"	D
110	"That Boy-Child of Mary"	F	355	"For All the Saints"	G
112	"He Is Born"	F	362	"Baptized in Water"	B♭
127	"The King of Glory Comes"	Em	366	"Let Us Break Bread Together"	E♭
143	"What Wondrous Love Is This"	Dm	370	"This Is a Day of New Beginnings"	E♭
152	"Christmas Has Its Cradle"	Dm	376	"We Meet Within This Holy Place"	F
157	"Worthy Is the Lamb"	G	377	"Jesus, at Your Holy Table"	F

NO.	TITLE	KEY	NO.	TITLE	KEY
383	"We Are God's People"	F	557	"People Need the Lord"	C
392	"Stir Your Church, O God, Our Father"	G	562	"When Christ Was Lifted from the Earth"	D
396	"When the Church of Jesus"	Dm	567	"Share His Love"	G
397	"Sing, Congregation, Sing"	C	579	"Shine, Jesus, Shine"	A♭
420	"I Will Trust in the Lord"	G	586	"We've a Story to Tell"	E♭
423	"Though I May Speak with Bravest Fire"	G	590	"God, Our Author and Creator"	A
433	"Rejoice in the Lord Always"	F	594	"Lift High the Cross"	C
435	"When in Our Music God Is Glorified"	G	597	"Here Am I, Send Me"	D
442	"Of All the Spirit's Gifts to Me"	D	599	"We Praise You with Our Minds, O Lord"	E♭
454	"God, Our Father, You Have Led Us"	E♭	602	"Jesus Was a Loving Teacher"	G
460	"When I Pray"	D	605	"Because I Have Been Given Much"	A♭
462	"The Lord's Prayer"	B♭	622	"Holy Lord"	F
465	"I Want Jesus to Walk with Me"	Cm	642	"Thanksgiving/Thanks-living"	G
487	"Stand Up, Stand Up for Jesus"	F	648	"Go with God"	E♭
488	"I'm Just a Child"	C	657	"Go Out and Tell"	C
500	"God, Who Touches Earth with Beauty"	C	660	"Go Now in Peace"	C
501	"Jesu, Jesu, Fill Us with Your Love"	D	661	"Grace, Love, and Fellowship"	D
531	"Redeemed"	E♭	663	"Grace to You"	G
540	"Saved, Saved"	B♭	664	"Grace to You and Peace"	Dm
549	"Creator of the Universe"	F	665	"Praise Ye the Name of the Lord"	D

Hymns Sung as Rounds or in Canon

"Row, row, row your boat, Gently down the stream." What child hasn't sung that simple song? By the time you reached elementary school, you probably learned to sing it in rounds. You may not have understood how it all worked then. All you knew was that it made beautiful music and it was fun to sing. Rounds are still popular today with children, youth, and adults. In fact, your choir and congregation can sing numerous hymns and choruses as rounds or in canon. (Both terms mean the same thing.)

The Baptist Hymnal, 1991, and *The Christian Praise Hymnal* each contain seven hymns/choruses (there may be more) which may be sung as rounds. To sing a round, divide the choir or congregation into as many parts as there are phrases in the music. (Most hymns in the hymnal will indicate the phrases with a number in a circle.) Assign each group of the choir or congregation to a specific phrase. In a round, one group begins singing, joined at a certain point by a second group which begins the melody again; when the second group reaches the same point, a third group begins the melody, continuing until all groups have entered. Upon reaching the end of the last phrase, each group may drop out or return to the beginning of the melody. In these hymns, the entrance or beginning point for each group is indicated by a number in a circle. (There is one exception.) In addition to being fun to sing, rounds are useful when teaching part singing to any choir member.

Rounds in these hymnals which are not identified in an index are as follows:

NO.	TITLE	PARTS	NO.	TITLE	PARTS
234	"King of Kings"	2	645	"Praise and Thanksgiving"	3
256	"Father, I Adore You" (not marked in hymnal)	3	660	"Go Now in Peace"	3
433	"Rejoice in the Lord Always"	3	664	"Grace to You and Peace"	3
622	"Holy Lord"	3			

Rounds may be sung in unison or in parts. The round will make its own harmony either way. It may be accompanied or unaccompanied. Here's how to set up a three-part round. This outline can be used for any round.

622   "Holy Lord"   Three-part round sung in unison. Divide choir or congregation into three groups; use the following pattern to sing this hymn. Three soloists may also be used rather than a choir.

	1	2	3		
Group 1:	1	2	3		
Group 2:		1	2	3	
Group 3:			1	2	3

Pentatonic Hymns

Hymns can be written in many different ways. While most are written in a major key, some are written in a minor key. Major and minor simply refer to a specific arrangement of notes in a scale. Major keys will have a series of whole steps and half steps arranged like the example below. All major keys will have this same arrangement of whole and half steps. Look at hymn 495, "Serve the Lord with Gladness," in the key of C. Here's a C **Major** scale.

Minor keys, likewise, have specific arrangements of whole and half steps which give minor keys their distinctive sound. Look again at the C major scale above. Now look at a **C Minor** scale below and see how they compare. Look at hymn 465, "I Want Jesus to Walk with Me," in the key of C minor. Here's a C **Minor scale**.

While several hymns sound minor, they are actually written in one of the ancient church modes. They are **modal** rather than minor because of a different arrangement of whole steps and half steps in their scale arrangement.

There is yet another scale in which some hymns may be found: the **pentatonic scale**. This scale consists of five notes. Pentatonic hymns have tunes—be they major, minor, or modal—which use a specific five-note pattern or scale. One of the more common forms of pentatonic scales omits the fourth and seventh degrees of the scale.

Hymn 330, "Amazing Grace! How Sweet the Sound," is written in the key of G major. The **G Major scale** looks like this: G A B C D E F♯ G.

The melody of this hymn, however, is pentatonic because it consists of only five different notes of the scale, omitting the fourth and seventh scale degrees. Here are the notes of the melody of this hymn:

```
D G    B–G  B      A    G    E    D
A - MAZ - ING  GRACE! HOW SWEET THE SOUND,

D    G      B–G  B      A    D
THAT SAVED  A    WRETCH LIKE ME!

B  D   B  D–B  G    D    E   G  G–E  D
I ONCE WAS LOST, BUT NOW  AM  FOUND,

D    G      B–G  B    A   G
WAS BLIND  BUT NOW  I   SEE.
```

Count the number of *different* notes in this melody (not the total). You'll find that from the G major scale, the following notes are used:

G A B D E

Did you notice that the fourth (C) and seventh (F♯) scale degrees were not used in this scale? Any five-note scale which omits the fourth and seventh scale degrees is a pentatonic scale. The pentatonic hymns in *The Baptist Hymnal,* 1991, and *The Christian Praise Hymnal* all utilize this type of five-note scale arrangement.

Identifying pentatonic hymns requires no special skill, just a sharp eye and ear. Simply check the melody (the part sopranos usually sing). If it does not have the fourth and seventh notes of the scale, it's pentatonic.

Pentatonic hymns are easy to play. A pianist can play any pentatonic hymn on all the black keys of the keyboard. A handbell choir, ringing only the bells of the pentatonic scale, may ring all the bells at once or in any sequence in order to play or accompany a pentatonic hymn. Children's choirs can also use a variety of instruments to accompany pentatonic hymns.

Here's a list of pentatonic hymns found in the two referenced hymnals.

NO.	TITLE	KEY	NO.	TITLE	KEY
330	"Amazing Grace! How Sweet the Sound"	G	489	"Lord, I Want to Be a Christian"	E♭
379	"Brethren, We Have Met to Worship"	A♭	59	"My Lord Is Near Me All the Time"	E♭
604	"Come, All Christians, Be Committed"	G	135	"Nothing but the Blood"	G
95	"Go, Tell It on the Mountain"	G	317	"Only Trust Him"	G
338	"How Firm a Foundation"	A♭	469	"Revive Us Again"	G
305	"I Have Decided to Follow Jesus"	D♭	566	"Tell the Good News"	F
418	"I've Got Peace Like a River"	G	142	"There Is a Fountain"	C
309	"Lord, I'm Coming Home"	A♭	156	"Were You There"	E♭
211	"I Love Thee"	E♭	522	"When the Morning Comes"	E♭
344	"Jesus Loves Me"	D			

Mastering the Metrical Mystery

Have you ever wondered about that mysterious string of numbers found beneath every hymn in *The Baptist Hymnal*, 1991, or *The Christian Praise Hymnal*, not to mention other hymnal editions? It's not a secret code; it's a metrical guide to the hymn. An understanding of these numbers can help you to utilize the hymns in your hymnal in some unique and creative ways. Let's see if we can unravel the mystery and help you to master the Metrical Index of your hymnal.

First an exercise is in order. Let's begin with two familiar hymns, "Praise God, from Whom All Blessings Flow" (more familiarly known as the "Doxology"), No. 253, and "Amazing Grace! How Sweet the Sound," No. 330. Open your hymnal to No. 253. *Count the total number of notes in each phrase of the melody.* Your findings should correspond with the numbers *above* the text in the following example:

THE "DOXOLOGY"

```
 1   2   3    4  5  6    7  8
Praise God, from whom all bless - ings flow;
 1   2   3    4  5  6    7  8
```

```
 1    2  3  4    5   6  7    8
Praise Him, all crea - tures here be - low;
 1    2  3  4    5   6  7    8
```

```
 1   2   3    4   5   6    7  8
Praise Him a - bove, ye heav 'n - ly host;
 1   2   3    4   5   6    7  8
```

```
 1   2   3   4   5 6  7    8
Praise Fa - ther, Son, and Ho - ly Ghost.
 1   2   3   4   5 6  7    8
```

"AMAZING GRACE! HOW SWEET THE SOUND"

```
 1   2   3-4  5    6    7    8  9
A - maz - ing grace!  how sweet the sound,
 1   2   3    4    5    6    7  8
```

```
 1    2   3-4  5     6    7
That saved  a  wretch like me!
 1    2   3    4     5    6
```

```
 1 2-3 4-5  6    7   8-9  10-11  12
I once was lost, but  now  am  found,
 1 2   3    4    5    6    7    8
```

```
  1    2   3-4  5   6 7
Was blind, but now I see.
  1    2   3    4   5 6
```

You should have counted a total of eight notes in the melody of each phrase of the "Doxology." Now go back and count the **total number of words and syllables in each phrase.** Again you will find there are eight. **From this count we arrive at the string of numbers found at the end of each hymn.** The metric indication for this hymn is 8.8.8.8. (L.M.)

As you will see in the next hymn (No. 330), the total number of notes in each phrase of the melody and the total number of words and syllables in each phrase may not always be the same.

The total number of notes in each phrase of the melody looks like 9.7.12.7. But remember, it's not the number of notes in the melody on which the metrical form of the hymn is based; hymn metrical form is based on the text or poetry of the hymn. Look again at the numbers beneath each phrase of the hymn. Those numbers are 8.6.8.6., meaning there are eight words or syllables in the first phrase, six in the second, eight in the third, and six in the fourth.

Here's a good working definition of meter as it is used in the language of hymns: **Meter—the number of syllables in a line or phrase of poetry.**

Next, look at the letters which are part of some hymn metric designations. Those hymns which have a meter of 8.8.8.8. are commonly referred to as Long Meter (L.M.) hymns. Those which have a meter of 8.6.8.6. are referred to as Common Meter (C.M.). Those having a metrical designation of 6.6.8.6. are known as Short Meter (S.M.) hymns. Those metrical indications ending with a "D." simply indicate that the pattern is doubled or repeated in hymns having eight-line/phrase stanzas. These are the three most commonly used meters in English hymnody.

Now turn to page 749. This is the Metrical Index of Tunes. In this index hymns are grouped by meter under columns headed by the various meters found in the hymnal, beginning with the smallest metrical designation of 2.2.2. and continuing to the largest—12.11.12.12. The final portion of this index contains hymns designated as *Irregular*. These hymns have no regularly recurring pattern of syllables in the lines or phrases of the text. This group is the largest of the entire index, containing more hymn listings than the other meters combined.

Perhaps you're saying to yourself, "OK. I now understand more about the meter of the hymns, but how can I use it in congregational worship?"

Look again at the Metrical Index of Tunes on page 749 in your hymnal. Look under the heading 8.6.8.6. (C.M.) There are 19 entries under this heading. *In theory*, it should be possible to swap or exchange any text and tune under this heading. However, *in practice* it may not always work, or at least may require slight modification. Let's examine two instances where hymn texts and tunes can be swapped effectively. Keep in mind that as the music leader, much of what is done with hymns metrically will be dictated by your own taste. Each hymn has its own character and style. The best metric swaps are those hymns which are similar in style.

From the heading 8.6.8.6. (C.M.) in the Metrical Index of Tunes, find the tune names CORONATION (202), NEW BRITAIN (330), and ST. ANNE (74). Look at NEW BRITAIN ("Amazing Grace! How Sweet the Sound") and ST. ANNE ("O God, Our Help in Ages Past"). You will notice immediately that both hymns are, musically, the same length. Now sing the text of "Amazing Grace!" to the tune of "O God, Our Help in Ages Past." How did it feel and sound? Is the text complemented by this new tune? Now try these two hymns in the reverse process, singing the text of "O God, Our Help in Ages Past" with the tune of "Amazing Grace!" How did you feel about this particular arrangement? Some may like it either way, while others may prefer a swap in only one direction. Again, your personal taste and preference will dictate how you choose to use this technique.

For another look at hymn metric swaps, let's again use the tune NEW BRITAIN. This time pair it with the tune CORONATION ("All Hail the Power of Jesus' Name"). A casual glance at these two hymns immediately reveals that one is twice as long as the other. Sing the text of "All Hail the Power of Jesus' Name" to the tune of "Amazing Grace!" Did you notice that you could only sing through about half the text? Reverse the process now. Sing the text of "Amazing Grace!" to the tune of "All Hail the Power of Jesus' Name." What did you have to do? You discovered that in order to finish the music, you had to repeat the final two lines/phrases of the text (or the entire last line of the hymn). Was it a compatible swap? Did you like it? Could your congregation sing it?

Swapping texts and tunes is a good way to introduce the text of an unfamiliar hymn to your congregation. Suppose your congregation does not know hymn 104, "See, to Us a Child Is Born," (tune name INNOCENTS) By consulting the Metrical Index under the heading 7.7.7.7. with its attendant variations, you'll discover that the tune CHINA, ("Jesus Loves Me," No. 344) is also in 7.7.7.7. meter but with an added refrain. Drop the refrain from this tune and you find that these two hymns can be effectively swapped.

In another example, consider hymn 590, "God, Our Author and Creator," (NALL AVENUE.) This is a beautiful hymn which has not yet been discovered by many music leaders and congregations. While it is not recommended that you avoid teaching your congregation new tunes, the hymn metric swap is one technique to use to at least introduce the text of a new hymn until the original music can be learned. You will note that this hymn has a meter of 8.7.8.7.D. Consulting the Metrical Index once again, you will find there are numerous selections of music which may be used with this hymn, including No. 62, "All the Way My Savior Leads Me" (Tune: ALL THE WAY); No. 398, "Glorious Things of Thee Are Spoken" (Tune: AUSTRIAN HYMN); and 613, "The Servant Song" (Tune: BEACH SPRING) to name a few.

You'll enjoy discovering all the possibilities for enhancing your congregational singing experience by employing the use of the hymn metric swap. Make a list of the swaps you like. There's a partial list already started on page 37. Add yours to this list.

Here are some things to consider as you make plans for employing this hymn-singing technique.

---

1. Don't use a hymn metric swap every week; it loses its effectiveness.

2. Make sure the congregation is familiar with both the text and the tune being swapped.

3. Be sure the music leader, the accompanists, and any other person or group that will lead in this effort are thoroughly rehearsed and know exactly what is being done; this is rehearsal work, and should never be done in front of the congregation. Play the music in the key written.

4. Make sure the hymns/tunes being swapped are compatible; determine beforehand whether a refrain will be dropped, or if a phrase will be repeated or deleted.

5. Provide the congregation with only the essential information they need to sing the hymns you lead; too much information can result in information overload, resulting in closed hymnbooks and spectators rather than participators.

6. Ask how this hymn metric swap will support the worship service. Will it enhance or detract? Will it create interest in singing, or a feeling of uneasiness? Does it go well with the general mood or direction of the service?

7. Remember the words *"in theory."* Don't try to force a match. Most of the swaps will work, but in those times when it will not, don't force it. Just accept the fact that it won't work and move on.

8. Occasionally a swap will be effective in one direction but not in the other. Use the direction that works and forget the other one.

9. Did I mention practice? Do it, and don't forget it.

Hymn metric swaps can breathe new life into tired, well-worn hymns. A swap can cause a congregation to come back "on line" during the hymn singing, causing them to consciously think about what they are singing.

The hymn metric swaps which follow feature a wide variety of possibilities. Two or more hymns are listed for each swap, with suggestions made for each set of hymns.

Hymn Metric Swaps

NO.	TITLE	TUNE	METER
118	"What Child Is This"	GREENSLEEVES	8.7.8.7. with refrain
188	"The Great Physician"	GREAT PHYSICIAN	8.7.8.7. with refrain

Suggestion: Use text of 188 with tune of 118; guitar or keyboard with string setting; drama suggested; reverse action not recommended.

552	"Jesus Is the Song"	SIMPSON	8.8.8.6. with refrain
303	"Just As I Am"	TABERNACLE	8.8.8.6.
542	"In Loving-Kindness Jesus Came"	HE LIFTED ME	8.8.8.6. with refrain

Suggestion: Use music of 552 (omit refrain) with text of 303 as invitational solo; or with text of 542; reverse action not recommended.

| 634 | "My Country, 'Tis of Thee" | AMERICA | 6.6.4.6.6.6.4. |
| 247 | "Come, Thou Almighty King" | ITALIAN HYMN | 6.6.4.6.6.6.4. |

Suggestion: Use text of 247 with tune of 634, with stately tempo; reverse action possible but not desirable.

| 56 | "Guide Me, O Thou Great Jehovah" | CWM RHONDDA | 8.7.8.7.8.7.7. |
| 94 | "Angels, from the Realms of Glory" | REGENT SQUARE | 8.7.8.7.8.7. |

Suggestion: Use text of 56 with tune of 94 (last line/phrase of text will be deleted); to reverse, repeat the last line/phrase of text of 94.

| 371 | "I Come with Joy to Meet My Lord" | LAND OF REST | 8.6.8.6. (C.M.) |
| 216 | "O for a Thousand Tongues to Sing" | AZMON | 8.6.8.6. (C.M.) |

Suggestion: This pair may be swapped easily in either direction with no modifications; use as call to worship.

453 . . . . "How Sweet the Name of Jesus Sounds . . . . ORTONVILLE . . . . 8.6.8.6. (C.M.)
217 . . . . "Oh, How I Love Jesus" . . . . OH, HOW I LOVE JESUS . . . 8.6.8.6. (C.M.)/refrain

Suggestion: Use as unit of medley on topic of the name of Jesus; use text of 453 with tune of 217, omitting last line/phrase of text of 453; use text of 217 with tune of 453, repeating last line/phrase of text just prior to refrain; sing refrain with either version of this swap.

480 . . . . "Immortal Love, Forever Full" . . . . SERENITY . . . . 8.6.8.6. (C.M.)
510 . . . . "O Lord, May Church and Home Combine" . . . . LAND OF REST . . . . 8.6.8.6. (C.M.)

Suggestion: Use text of 510 with tune of 480 to create a prayer-like hymn for Christian Home Emphasis; may be used in either direction.

630 . . . . "America the Beautiful" . . . . MATERNA . . . . 8.6.8.6.D. (C.M.D.)
 93 . . . . "It Came upon the Midnight Clear" . . . . CAROL . . . . 8.6.8.6.D. (C.M.D.)

Suggestion: Use text of 630 with tune of 93 as an alternate tune for patriotic service; may be sung by soloist or choir; may be sung in either direction, but perhaps not as effective in reverse.

137 . . . . "O Sacred Head, Now Wounded" . . . . PASSION CHORALE . . . . 7.6.7.6.D.
276 . . . . "O Jesus, I Have Promised" . . . . ANGEL'S STORY . . . . 7.6.7.6.D.

Suggestion: Many congregations, and their music leaders, do not know or sing 137; introduce this text by singing it to the tune of 276, a more familiar hymn; also effective in reverse.

262 . . . . "Word of God, Across the Ages" . . . . AUSTRIAN HYMN . . . . 8.7.8.7.D.
590 . . . . "God, Our Author and Creator" . . . . NALL AVENUE . . . . 8.7.8.7.D.

Suggestion: Use the more familiar tune of 262 to introduce the new text of 590; also effective in reverse.

223 . . . . "Alleluia" . . . . ALLELUIA . . . . 8.8.8.8. (L.M.)
182 . . . . "What a Friend We Have in Jesus" . . . . CONVERSE . . . . 8.7.8.7.D.
 15 . . . . "Come, Thou Fount of Every Blessing" . . . . NETTLETON . . . . 8.7.8.7.D.
 61 . . . . "Savior, Like a Shepherd Lead Us" . . . . BRADBURY . . . . 8.7.8.7.D.

Suggestion: Use the tune of 223 to sing the first stanza text of 182, 15, and 61 in succession; choice: sing the first two lines of each hymn, or sing the tune of 223 twice to complete the first stanza text. Although this crossover of meters is unusual, it does work in the manner indicated; not recommended for use in reverse.

 56 . . . . "Guide Me, O Thou Great Jehovah" . . . . CWM RHONDDA . . . . 8.7.8.7.8.7.7.
 80 . . . . "Let All Mortal Flesh Keep Silence" . . . . PICARDY . . . . 8.7.8.7.8.7.

Suggestion: Because of the modification/alteration required, this is not recommended for congregational use; appropriate for soloist or choral use; use text of 56 with tune of 80; delete one of the repeated phrases on third line of hymn ("Bread of heaven" in stanza one, for instance); effective in service on themes of providence, God the Father, and so forth.

Music has often been called a "language of worship." Henry van Dyke described music as "worship putting on her garment of praise." Music for the congregation is the hymn—the backbone of church music. Hymn singing likely is the only chance the congregation has for active musical participation in the service. The congregation is the most important music group in the church. This being true, it seems that a proportionate amount of time should be spent planning for congregational music activities in worship.

James Rawlings Sydnor, in *Hymns and Their Uses*, lists five values of hymn singing. They are values every church music leader should know and seek to impart to others. "Through hymn singing," Sydnor writes, "Christians express their feelings and ideas . . . tell others what they believe . . . are bound in closer fellowship . . . are instructed in the fundamentals of their faith . . . [and] are sustained in daily life."[1] Should it ever be necessary to validate what we do as music ministers, surely the imparting of these values to others would suffice.

Several years ago while preparing for a Thanksgiving service, I came across a litany (a reading) and a new hymn my congregation didn't know. I wanted to use both of these items in the service, but knew the congregation would bog down without preparation. So, during the month preceding Thanksgiving, I conducted a congregational rehearsal during the mid-week prayer service and just prior to each Sunday evening service. The reading began just as a typical responsive reading would begin: dull and monotonous, with little or no inflection in the voice. The hymn began much the same as any new hymn does: the music leader sings it as a solo until the congregation gradually learns it. During the course of the month, however, with patience and constant rehearsal, the congregation soon began to read and sing with feeling and expressiveness. By the time Thanksgiving came, they were so excited they could hardly wait. When it came time to do these two items in the service, they were magnificent. I learned a valuable lesson that day: if we wish for the congregation to have meaningful times of worship through music as participants rather than spectators, we must find ways to help them prepare for worship. Preparation takes time and energy, but the results are well worth it. Come to think of it, it's the least we can do.

There's one final consideration which must be addressed relative to congregational music: the topic of new music. Most people have comfort zones of church music and, for that matter, other kinds of music as well. Tampering with their comfort zone or approaching it in the wrong manner can land an unaware or insensitive music leader in hot water fast. Most people are quick to express their opinions, too. There's not one of us who hasn't heard the phrase, "I don't like that music!"

An appropriate reply to those who "don't like that music" might be to remind them that at some point in their lives, every piece of music was brand new, yet they learned and continue to learn many new songs. It takes patience and perseverance.

Writing about introducing new music to the church, Robert H. Mitchell states that "the point here is that both acceptance of reality, and commitment to unusual effort must characterize any such new endeavor."[2] His premise is that any attempt at introducing something new must be done with the highest level of competence and ability. In the language of business, we are doing a marketing and selling job on a new hymn or other piece of music. If we want to "sell" it, it must have our very best promotional effort.

Mitchell further states that "It is not essential that we agree on all matters of faith and practice. It is essential that we learn to handle lack of agreement in a Christian manner. Matters of individual preference should not be concealed or ignored. They should be identified and explored in order that mutual growth may take place. In summary," he continues, "If you like the music, enjoy it! If you don't care for the music, be patient. Listen! You might come to like it. Someone does."[3]

Spend some time considering those music activities which would be meaningful to your congregation, then help them prepare to experience a new level of active worship participation. Here are some ideas which can help.

1. Get a personal copy of the hymnal for your exclusive use. Mark the hymnal as you would your Bible, with helpful information on leading the hymn, music information, unusual words or phrases, and anything that will aid you in planning and leading congregational hymn singing.

2. Become familiar with the layout of the hymnal: its four grand divisions of hymns, including the Scripture readings on the divider pages between subdivisions; its worship aids; and its indexes. A good working

knowledge of the contents can help you immensely as you plan for worship.

3. As you lead a hymn, know whom you are addressing in the hymn. Most hymns speak to one or more persons or groups. Hymns may be addressed to God, to believers, and to nonbelievers. Some address God's creations other than people, while others address God in three Persons, or the Trinity.

4. Introduce new hymns as an exciting new way to meet God or to express our praise to Him. Too many music leaders either dismiss the importance of singing new hymns or simply fail to learn them. The Hymn-of-the-Month Plan is a good method to use when introducing new or unfamiliar hymns.

5. Make a list of hymns which could be used as solos, duets, trios, quartets, or sung by some group other than the choir. Enlist people to sing one or more of these hymns in a worship service. Post a quarterly schedule of worship music assignments. Update it regularly. Begin by using hymns from the Testimony section of the hymnal (numbers 530 through 555).

6. Create a list of hymns which can be sung antiphonally (that is, with an echo group). For instance, "Come, Christians, Join to Sing" (No. 231) may be sung in this fashion. Have one group, perhaps the congregation, sing the first phrase ("Come, Christians, join to sing") followed by the choir singing the second phrase ("Alleluia, Amen!") Other good hymns for using this technique include "All Creatures of Our God and King" (No. 27), and "How Great Our Joy" (No. 108).

7. In addition to the hymns listed in the section on rounds, other hymns can be sung in canon (unaccompanied) at a distance of one measure. In other words, the second group begins when the first group has completed the first measure. Have everyone sing the complete stanza or hymn first, then in canon. These hymns include No. 44, "For the Beauty of the Earth"; No. 330, "Amazing Grace! How Sweet the Sound"; No. 338, "How Firm a Foundation"; No. 68, "My Shepherd Will Supply My Need"; No. 371, "I Come with Joy to Meet My Lord"; No. 510, "O Lord, May Church and Home Combine"; No. 517, "Jerusalem, My Happy Home"; No. 355, "For All the Saints"; and No. 323, "Come, Ye Sinners, Poor and Needy."

8. Consider reading a stanza of a hymn rather than singing it. The absence of music for one stanza can often turn total attention to the text.

9. Sing an entire hymn *a cappella*. The effect can be dramatic.

10. Build a hymn service on one selected passage of Scripture. Consult the Scriptural Bases for Hymns Index on page 737. Ask your pastor to provide the Scripture passage for a service as far in advance as possible to allow time for adequate preparation and planning on your part and that of the choir and other groups.

11. Dramatize a hymn. Using simple materials, enlist those who have some dramatic talent or ability and who are able to memorize lines. Numerous materials are available on hymn dramas, including *The Church Musician*. The *Handbook to The Baptist Hymnal* provides excellent background information on the hymns.

12. Present a hymn monologue. Enlist someone to memorize a brief monologue and let him tell the story of the hymn or hymn writer during a worship service. Consider enlisting several persons to prepare monologues for future use.

13. Have a Hymn Writer of the Quarter service. Once per quarter, plan a special evening music service featuring the hymns and life story of a particular hymn writer. B. B. McKinney, Charlotte Elliott, Frances Havergal, and Fanny Crosby are some good ones with which to begin. Don't forget about more contemporary hymn writers. There are lots of them in the hymnal. Sing the music of one or several during a special service or program.

14. Have a Hymn Writer Day. Invite a contemporary hymn writer to visit your church and lead in the hymn singing. He or she may also give a testimony or the story behind the hymns. They may also be commissioned to write a hymn for your church, or a hymn arrangement for the choir, or they might suggest a composer for their hymn text.

15. Create a hymn medley on a specific theme or topic.

16. Create a hymn metric swap.

17. Have a Sermon in Song. For instance, there is a sufficient number of hymns on the Life of Christ. Such a service might have as headings "Birth," "Boyhood," "Life and Ministry," "Suffering and Death," and

"Resurrection." Select appropriate stanzas from hymns to support the headings.

18. Have a time of Singspiration or a Favorite Hymn Night. Allow the congregation to select the hymns to be sung. Sing fewer stanzas of each to allow time for more selections. An option might be to ask the person making the request to share why this hymn is her favorite.

19. Use alternative accompaniment within one hymn. For instance, use the piano on one stanza, the organ on another, perhaps both on yet another. If you have access to other keyboard, band, or orchestral instruments, plan for one or more of these to accompany the hymn. There are instrumental editions of the hymnal for every instrument of the orchestra.

20. Plan a special Hymnal Dedication Service if the hymnal is still fairly new in your church. Many churches have already done this and would be glad to share a copy of their program for ideas in creating your own.

21. Plan a Sing-Through-the-Hymnal emphasis, possibly in conjunction with a Read-the-Bible-Through. This could be done during the course of a year.

22. Enlist a capable soloist to offer a prayer in song on behalf of the congregation. With the congregation bowed in prayer, a soloist might sing No. 455, "I Must Tell Jesus"; No. 568, "Lord, Speak to Me, That I May Speak"; No. 603, "My Singing Is a Prayer"; No. 281, "Speak to My Heart"; or No. 462, "The Lord's Prayer."

23. Don't forget the children. *The Baptist Hymnal,* 1991, and *The Christian Praise Hymnal* both have numerous hymns for children. Consider using a children's choir or child soloist to sing No. 488, "I'm Just a Child," or No. 610, "What Can I Give Him," during a Parent/Child Dedication Day or on the theme of Stewardship.

24. Analyze the hymns your congregation sings during a one-year period. The *Music Ministry Plan Book*, published annually by the Music Department of the Baptist Sunday School Board, contains hymn sheets which allow you to record the use of every hymn in the hymnal, including hymns used in the Sunday morning service, Sunday evening service, weekday service, choral use, revival service, solo or ensemble use, or as an invitation hymn. There's also a place to tally the totals. If you've never done this, it might surprise you to learn how few different hymns many churches actually sing.

25. Ask your pastor to preach from the hymnal occasionally. The hymnal is full of theology and tenets of the faith. The Scripture reference tied to each hymn makes it especially convenient to develop sermon ideas and thoughts. Other material helps are also available from various sources.

---

[1]James Rawlings Sydnor, *Hymns & Their Uses: A Guide to Improved Congregational Singing* (Carol Stream, IL: AGAPE, 1982), 16-21.

[2]Robert H. Mitchell, *I Don't Like That Music* (Carol Stream, IL: Hope Publishing Company, 1993), 118.

[3]Ibid., 131.

Personal Learning Activities

From "Suggestions for Worship Planning"

1. What is a worship leader?

   _____

2. Who are worship leaders?

   _____
   _____

3. Name six suggestions for worship planning.

   _____
   _____
   _____
   _____
   _____
   _____

From "Themes for Worship"

1. List 15 worship themes.

   _____   _____
   _____   _____
   _____   _____
   _____   _____
   _____   _____
   _____   _____
   _____   _____
   _____

2. Identify at least 10 worship themes which have been used in your church during the past six months.

   _____   _____
   _____   _____
   _____   _____
   _____   _____
   _____   _____

From "Suggestions for Using the Worship Worksheet"

1. Write a brief paragraph describing how you would use the Worship Worksheet.

   _____
   _____
   _____

From "Hymn Treatments"

1. What is a hymn treatment?

   _____
   _____

2. Select a favorite hymn of yours and "treat" it.

_____

_____

_____

_____

_____

From "Hymn Medleys"

1. What is a hymn medley?

_____

_____

2. What are some purposes for using a hymn medley in worship?

_____

_____

3. List the eight-step process for creating a medley.

_____

_____

_____

_____

_____

_____

_____

4. Why is it unwise to have the congregation sing a very long medley? What are some solutions?

_____

_____

_____

5. Create a hymn medley consisting of three hymns and a chorus.

_____

_____

_____

_____

From "Some things You Wanted to Know About Modulations but Were Afraid to Ask"

1. What is a modulation?

_____

2. What are some ways modulations can be effectively used?

_____

_____

3. What is the easiest modulation technique?

_____

_____

_____

4. Explain the use of the modulation chart from the hymnal found on pages 24 and 25 of this book.

_____

_____

_____

5. Create a hymn medley of at least three hymns in different keys, and show the modulation process of your choice.

_____

_____

_____

From "Hymns of Ethnic Origin"
1. List some ways in which hymns of ethnic origins might be used in a worship service.

_____

_____

_____

From "Hymns of African-American Tradition or Origin"
1. List five hymns of African-American tradition or origin.

_____

_____

_____

_____

_____

2. Create a medley of at least three hymns from this tradition.

_____

_____

_____

_____

From "Hymns Written in Unison (All or Part)"
1. What are some uses of unison hymns?

_____

_____

_____

From "Hymns Sung as Rounds or in Canon"
1. What is a round?

_____

_____

2. How can a round be taught to the choir? To the congregation?

_____

_____

_____

3. List three hymns which can be sung unaccompanied at a distance of one measure?

_____

_____

_____

From "Pentatonic Hymns"
1. What is a pentatonic scale? Write the pentatonic scale in the key of C.

_____

_____

_____

2. List four pentatonic hymns.

_____

_____

_____

_____

_____

From "Mastering the Metrical Mystery"
1. What is the difference between the time signature and the meter of a hymn?

_____

_____

2. Is the meter of a hymn related to the music or to the text?

_____

_____

3. Identify the following by giving word definition and metric designation.
   L.M. _____
   C.M. _____
   S.M. _____
   D.   _____
4. What is meant by the term *irregular meter*?

_____

_____

5. What are some things to consider when employing the use of the hymn metric swap?

_____

_____

_____

6. What do the words *in theory* mean with regard to working with the metrical index?

_____

_____

From "Getting the Most from Your Hymnal"
1. What is a good way of introducing new music to the congregation?

_____

_____

_____

2. What are five values of hymn singing?

_____
_____
_____
_____
_____

3. From the list of 25 ideas for congregational music activities, which three might you consider using in your church during the next year?

_____
_____
_____

The Church Study Course

The Church Study Course System is a Southern Baptist educational system designed to support leadership training and Christian development. This system provides courses, recognition, record keeping, and regular reports for participants and churches

This system is characterized by short courses ranging from 2½ to 10 hours in length. They may be studied individually or in groups. With more than 600 courses in 24 subject areas, it offers diploma/certificate plans in all areas of church leadership and Christian growth.

With the heart of the system being leadership training, courses are available for adults and youth. Youth may earn credit on any course in the system, but some are especially designed for them. Noncredit courses for children and preschoolers are also available.

The Church Study Course serves all church programs and is jointly sponsored by many agencies within the Southern Baptist Convention. Sponsors include: Baptist Sunday School Board, Woman's Missionary Union, Brotherhood Commission, Home Mission Board, Stewardship Commission, and the respective departments of the state conventions and associations affiliated with the Southern Baptist Convention.

How to Request Credit for this Course

This book is the text for course number 10089 in the subject area Church Music. Credit for this course may be obtained two ways:

1. Read the book and attend class sessions. (If you are absent from one or more sessions, complete the "Personal Learning Activities" for the material missed.)

2. Read the book and complete the "Personal Learning Activities." (Written work should be submitted to an appropriate church leader.)

A request for credit may be made on Form 725 "Church Study Course Enrollment/Credit Request" and sent to Church Study Course Resources Section, MSN 117, Baptist Sunday School Board, 127 Ninth Avenue North, Nashville, Tennessee 37234. The form below may be used to request credit. Enrollment in a diploma plan also may be made on Form 725.

Each person with Church Study Course activity during the previous 12 months will receive a complete up-to-date report called a transcript. Transcripts will be mailed to churches for distribution to members in the September-November quarter (available on request at other times.) Consult the latest Church Study Course catalog for complete details.

CHURCH STUDY COURSE ENROLLMENT/CREDIT REQUEST
FORM - 725 (Rev.1/93)

MAIL THIS REQUEST TO CHURCH STUDY COURSE RESOURCES SECTION
BAPTIST SUNDAY SCHOOL BOARD
127 NINTH AVENUE, NORTH
NASHVILLE, TENNESSEE 37234

Is this the first course taken since 1983? ☐ **YES** If yes, or not sure complete all of Section 1. ☐ **No** If no, complete only bold boxes in Section 1.

SECTION 1 - STUDENT I.D.

Social Security Number | Personal CSC Number*

☐ Mr ☐ Miss / ☐ Mrs. ☐   DATE OF BIRTH ▶ Month Day Year

Name (First, MI, Last)

Street, Route, or P.O.Box

City, State | Zip Code

Church Name

Mailing Address

City, State | Zip Code

SECTION 2 CHANGE REQUEST ONLY (Current Inf. in Section 1)

☐ Former Name

☐ Former Address | Zip Code

☐ Former Church | Zip Code

SECTION 3 - COURSE CREDIT REQUEST

Course No.	Title (Use exact title)
1. **10089**	**The Volunteer/Bivocational Music Leader: A Guide to Using the Hymnal Creatively**
2.	
3.	
4.	
5.	
6.	

SECTION 4 - DIPLOMA/CERTIFICATE ENROLLMENT

Enter exact diploma/certificate title from current Church Study Course catalog. Indicate age group/or area if appropriate. Do not enroll again with each course. When all requirements have been met, the diploma/certificate will be mailed to your church. Enrollment in Christian Development Diplomas is automatic. No charge will be made for enrollment or diplomas/certificates.

Title of Diploma/Certificate | Age group or area

Title of Diploma/Certificate | Age group or area

Signature of Pastor, Teacher, or Other Church Leader | Date

*CSC # not required for new students. Others please give CSC # when using SS # for the first time. Then, only one ID # is required. SS# and date of birth requested but not required.